Taking Care of Your

Centaur

Eric Braun

BLACK
RABBIT
BOOKS

Hi Jinx is published by Black Rabbit Books
P.O. Box 3263, Mankato, Minnesota, 56002.
www.blackrabbitbooks.com
Copyright © 2020 Black Rabbit Books

Marysa Storm, editor; Michael Sellner, designer;
Omay Ayres, photo researcher

Library of Congress Cataloging-in-Publication Data
Names: Braun, Eric, 1971- author, illustrator.
Title: Taking care of your centaur / by Eric Braun.
Description: Mankato, Minnesota : Black Rabbit Books, [2020]
Series: Hi Jinx. Caring for your magical pets | Summary:
Provides easy-to-read instructions for choosing and caring for
a pet centaur, and points out the trouble these half-human,
half-horses cause when bored. Includes discussion questions. |
Includes bibliographical references and index.
Identifiers: LCCN 2018043202 (print) | LCCN 2018052397
(ebook) | ISBN 9781680729153 (e-book) | ISBN 9781680729092
(library binding) | ISBN 9781644660881 (paperback)
Subjects: | CYAC: Centaurs–Fiction. | Pets–Fiction.
Classification: LCC PZ7.1.B751542 (ebook) | LCC PZ7.1.B751542
Tah 2020 (print) | DDC [E]–dc23
LC record available at https://lccn.loc.gov/2018043202

Printed in China. 1/19

Image Credits

Dreamstime: Insima, 12 (btm horse body, hay); iStock: 9lle, 7 (horse
body); Sergey Shambulin, 16–17 (pizza, human body), 22 (pizza, human
body); Tigatelu, 12 (blanket); zaricm, 12 (btm human body); Shutterstock:
Akulinina, 20 (liger); Alena Kozlova, 19 (bkgd); alexmstudio, 12 (top bkgd);
Aluna1, 7 (bkgd); Angeliki Vel, 19 (sun); benchart, 4 (bkgd); Danilo Sanino,
8–9; Denys Shmakov, 1 (horse body), 19 (horse body); DM7, 2–3; DVitaliy,
12 (btm bkgd); Freestyle_stock_photo, Cover (bkgd); GraphicsRF, 4 (horse
btm); HitToon, 12 (top horse btm), 21 (horse); KimMinThien, 16–17 (bkgd);
Lorelyn Medina, Cover (car wash), 15 (car wash); manas_ko, 4 (human body,
Frisbee), 5 (kid); mejnak, 4 (trees, clouds); Memo Angeles, Cover (centaur,
boy, water, hose), 1 (girl, human top), 4 (bunny), 7 (giraffe, zebra, human
top, butterfly), 9 (knight), 11 (all), 12 (kids), 15 (centaur, boy, water, hose),
18 (girl), 19 (human top); Okuneva, Back Cover (bkgd), 3 (bkgd), 12 (bkgd),
21 (bkgd); opicobello, 7 (marker strokes), 14 (tear), 17 (page tear); Pasko
Maksim, Back Cover (tear), 23, 24; Paul Brennan, 20 (zonkey); pitju, 10 (page
curl), 21 (page curl); Robynrg, 20 (mule); Ron Dale, 5 (marker stroke), 6, 13,
20 (marker stroke); Ron Leishman, 16, 17 (girl, wagon), 22 (boy); Sararoom
Design, 12 (top human top); Tueris, 18 (marker strokes); Victor Brave,
Cover (nozzle), 15 (nozzle); Willierossin, 16–17 (grass, horse body), 22
(grass, horse body); your, 15 (clouds) Every effort has been made to contact
copyright holders for material reproduced in this book. Any omissions will be
rectified in subsequent printings if notice is given to the publisher.

Contents

Chapter 1

Is a Centaur Right for You?

A centaur runs through a park on powerful legs. It leaps into the air. Using its human arms, it grabs a Frisbee. The centaur then whips the Frisbee back to its owner.

Centaurs are awesome pets. They're way better than dogs. You don't play fetch with centaurs. You play catch. You don't have to take them for boring walks either. You can ride them instead! Having a centaur is fun. But it takes work.

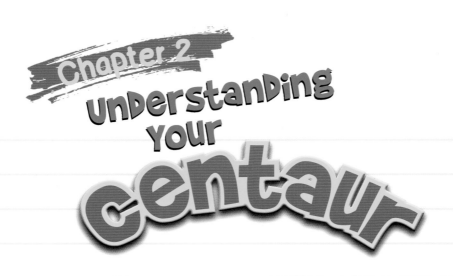

Chapter 2
Understanding Your Centaur

Before you get a centaur, you must understand them. Centaurs are horses with human **torsos**, heads, and arms. They are large and very strong. These creatures come from a magical land. So they might find your home boring. Bored centaurs can be trouble. They might destroy your belongings. Or they might prank you. You'll need to play with your centaur to keep it from getting into trouble.

Centaurs like playing with other animals. Your centaur should get along with any pets you already have.

There are many **ancient** stories about centaurs. These stories say centaurs are wild, rough troublemakers.

But that's not always true. Yes, some are wild. But many centaurs are gentle. Most are wise. Get to know your centaur. You might be surprised by how much you have in common.

A Close Relationship

Centaurs are different than other pets. You and your centaur can talk together. You can share secrets and jokes. You can become very close. But centaurs are proud and protective. They might become jealous if you have other close friends. Set rules early on. Remind your centaur that it's a pet.

Chapter 3
Caring for your Centaur

Caring for a centaur is a bit complicated. It isn't cheap either. You'll need a lot of outdoor space. Centaurs must have room to stretch their arms and legs. You'll also need a **stable** for your centaur to sleep in. It's best not to let this pet in the house. Its hooves will damage the floors.

You'll need to take your centaur to a human doctor and a vet. You'll probably need to take your centaur to the dentist too. Get your teeth cleaned together. It'll be fun!

Keeping Clean

Centaurs have arms and hands. That means they can clean themselves. But you have to remind them. Most centaurs don't care about being clean. Once a week, **encourage** your centaur to bathe. Take it to a car wash. Your centaur won't fit in the shower!

Eating and Exercising

Centaurs eat a lot. They like many of the same foods you do. They love veggie burgers. They can't get enough pizza. In fact, a centaur can eat 10 large pizzas in one meal. These foods are special treats, though. Make sure they eat mostly fruits and vegetables.

Put your centaur on your Ultimate Frisbee team. You are **guaranteed** to win. Just check the rules to make sure pets are allowed.

Centaurs also love exercising. They should get at least one hour of activity each day. Running is a great way for a centaur to work out.

A Lifelong Friend

There are a lot of things to consider when owning a centaur. They need attention, care, and lots of food. But owners say their centaurs are worth it. Take care of your centaur. And remember to have fun with it. It'll be a loving pet for many years.

Chapter 4
Get in on the
Hi Jinx

Centaurs don't really exist. But there are real combination animals. A liger is part lion and part tiger. Zonkeys are a cross between zebras and donkeys. One popular **hybrid** animal is the mule. It's a cross between a donkey and a horse. There are many hybrid animals. None of them are half human, though.

liger

mule

zonkey

Take It One Step More

1. Magical creatures are popular in movies and TV shows. Why do you think that is?

2. What sports do you think a centaur would be good at? What sports would be hard for it?

3. Invent your own creature by combining two different animals. What is your new creature called?

GLOSSARY

ancient (AYN-shunt)—from a time long ago

encourage (en-KUR-ij)—to make someone or something more likely to do something

guarantee (gar-uhn-TEE)—a promise or assurance

hybrid (HAHY-brid)—of mixed origin

stable (STAY-buhl)—a building where animals are sheltered

torso (TAWR-soh)—the human body except for the head, arms, and legs

BOOKS

Marsico, Katie. *Beastly Monsters: From Dragons to Griffins.* Monster Mania. Minneapolis: Lerner Publications, 2017.

Palmer, Erin. *Greek Mythology.* Mythology Marvels. Vero Beach, FL: Rourke Educational Media, 2017.

Randolph, Joanne ed. *The Myths and Legends of Ancient Greece and Rome.* Mythology and Legends Around the World. New York: Cavendish Square Publishing, 2018.

WEBSITES

Ancient Greece for Kids: Monsters and Creatures of Greek Mythology
www.ducksters.com/history/ancient_greece/ monsters_and_creatures_of_greek_mythology.php

Greek Mythology's Mystical Creatures
kids.nationalgeographic.com/explore/greek-mythology-s-mystical-creatures/

Herakles. Or Hercules. A Problematic Hero: Crash Course World Mythology #30
www.youtube.com/watch?v=R0qkSTvRQa8

INDEX